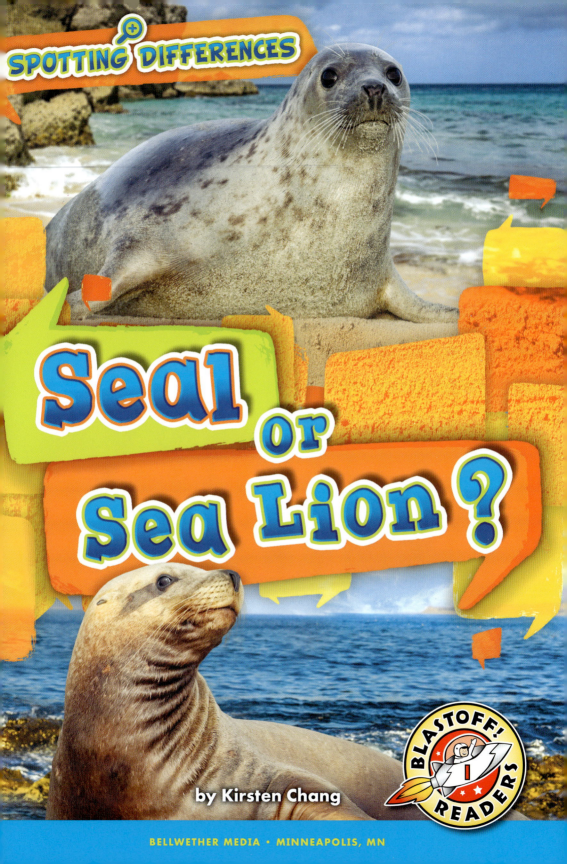

Blastoff! Readers are carefully developed by literacy experts to build reading stamina and move students toward fluency by combining standards-based content with developmentally appropriate text.

Level 1 provides the most support through repetition of high-frequency words, light text, predictable sentence patterns, and strong visual support.

Level 2 offers early readers a bit more challenge through varied sentences, increased text load, and text-supportive special features.

Level 3 advances early-fluent readers toward fluency through increased text load, less reliance on photos, advancing concepts, longer sentences, and more complex special features.

★ Blastoff! Universe

This edition first published in 2021 by Bellwether Media, Inc.

No part of this publication may be reproduced in whole or in part without written permission of the publisher. For information regarding permission, write to Bellwether Media, Inc., Attention: Permissions Department, 6012 Blue Circle Drive, Minnetonka, MN 55343.

Library of Congress Cataloging-in-Publication Data

Names: Chang, Kirsten, 1991- author.
Title: Seal or sea lion? / by Kirsten Chang.
Description: Minneapolis, MN : Bellwether Media, 2021. | Series: Blastoff readers : spotting differences | Includes bibliographical references and index. | Audience: Ages 5-8 | Audience: Grades K-3 | Summary: "Developed by literacy experts for students in kindergarten through grade three, this book introduces seals and sea lions to young readers through leveled text and related photos"-- Provided by publisher.
Identifiers: LCCN 2020035704 (print) | LCCN 2020035705 (ebook) | ISBN 9781644874059 (library binding) | ISBN 9781648340826 (ebook)
Subjects: LCSH: Seals (Animals)--Juvenile literature. | Sea lions--Juvenile literature.
Classification: LCC QL737.P63 C43 2021 (print) | LCC QL737.P63 (ebook) | DDC 599.79--dc23
LC record available at https://lccn.loc.gov/2020035704
LC ebook record available at https://lccn.loc.gov/2020035705

Text copyright © 2021 by Bellwether Media, Inc. BLASTOFF! READERS and associated logos are trademarks and/or registered trademarks of Bellwether Media, Inc.

Editor: Elizabeth Neuenfeldt   Designer: Laura Sowers

Printed in the United States of America, North Mankato, MN.

Table of Contents

Seals and Sea Lions	4
Different Looks	8
Different Lives	14
Side by Side	20
Glossary	22
To Learn More	23
Index	24

Seals and Sea Lions

Seals and sea lions are **mammals**. They have long **whiskers**.

These animals live on land and in water. How are they different?

seal

Different Looks

Sea lions have ear **flaps**. Seals have small ear holes.

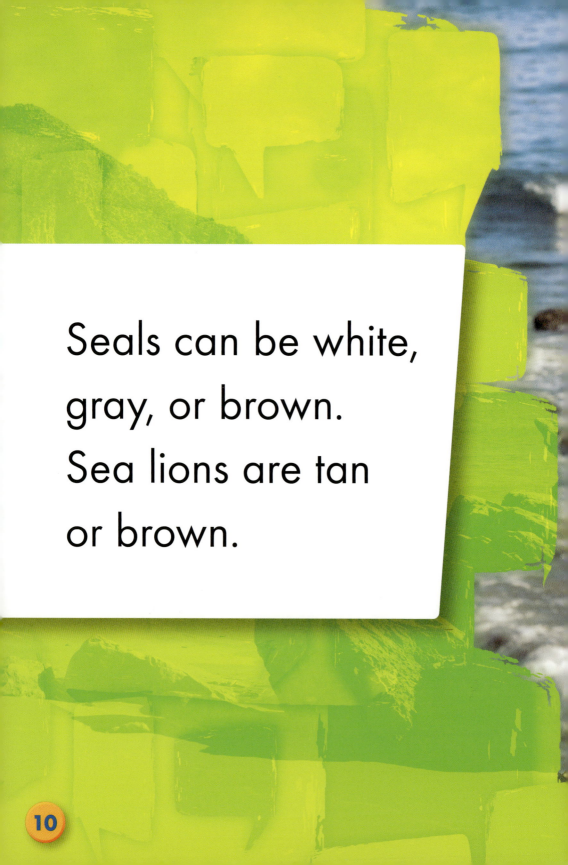

Seals can be white, gray, or brown. Sea lions are tan or brown.

Sea lions have large **flippers**. Seals have small flippers covered in fur.

flipper

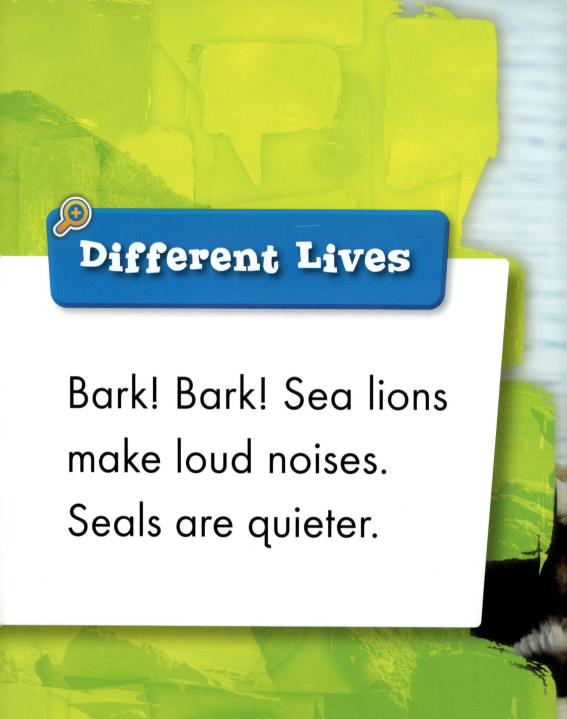

Different Lives

Bark! Bark! Sea lions make loud noises. Seals are quieter.

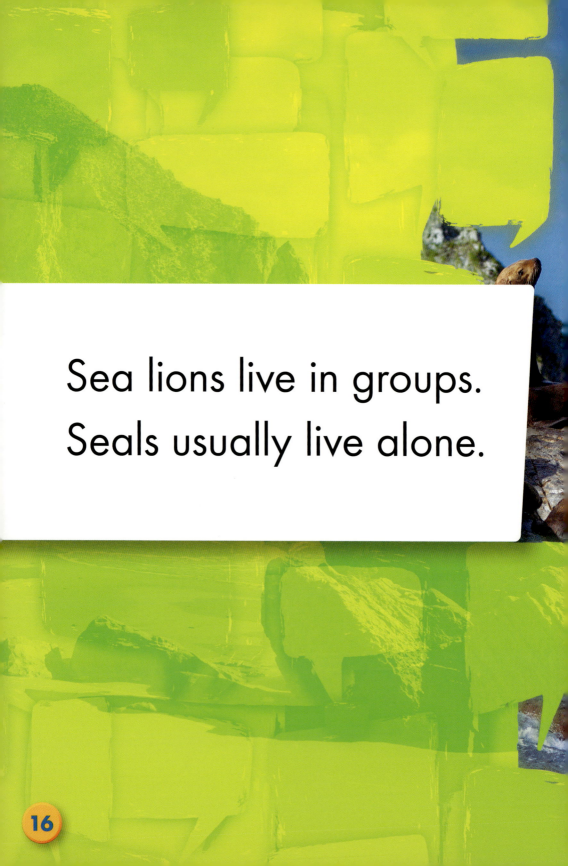

Sea lions live in groups. Seals usually live alone.

Seals mostly live in water. Sea lions spend more time on land. Which animal is this?

Side by Side

white, gray, or brown

small ear holes

small, fur-covered flippers

Seal Differences

live alone

make quiet noises

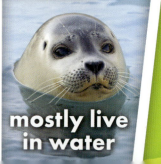

mostly live in water

Glossary

flaps — thin pieces of skin

mammals — warm-blooded animals that have hair and feed their young milk

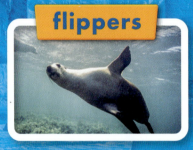

flippers — flat limbs that animals use to swim

whiskers — long, stiff hairs that grow near the mouths of some animals

To Learn More

AT THE LIBRARY

Arnold, Quinn M. *Seals*. Mankato, Minn.: Creative Education, 2017.

Bozzo, Linda. *How Seals Grow Up*. New York, N.Y.: Enslow Publishing, 2020.

Ryndak, Rob. *Seal or Sea Lion?* New York, N.Y.: Gareth Stevens Publishing, 2016.

ON THE WEB

FACTSURFER

Factsurfer.com gives you a safe, fun way to find more information.

1. Go to www.factsurfer.com.

2. Enter "seal or sea lion" into the search box and click 🔍.

3. Select your book cover to see a list of related content.

Index

colors, 10
ear flaps, 8, 9
ear holes, 8, 9
flippers, 12, 13
groups, 16
land, 6, 18
mammals, 4
noises, 14
water, 6, 18
whiskers, 4, 5

The images in this book are reproduced through the courtesy of: ujourd, cover (seal); KenCanning, cover (sea lion); RHIMAGE, pp. 4-5; slowmotiongli, pp. 6-7; Bjoern Wylezich, pp. 8-9; leungchopan, p. 9 (ear flap); Steve Bruckmann, pp. 10-11; JakIZdenek, p. 11 (seal); AndreAnita, pp. 12-13; gmeland, pp. 14-15; Atly, pp. 16-17; Ondrej Prosicky, pp. 18-19; Eric Isselee, pp. 20 (seal), 21 (sea lion); K Ireland, p. 20 (live alone); Ulrike Jordan, p. 20 (quiet); Steve Meese, p. 20 (water); Steve Allen, p. 21 (live in groups); A Life Beneath Stars, p. 21 (loud); Patrick Rolands, p. 21 (land); ArtDary, p. 22 (flaps); Vladimir Melnik, p. 22 (flippers); Iam D M Robertson, p. 22 (mammals); Sylvie Bouchard, p. 22 (whiskers).